First published 1998
by Hodder Children's Books,
a division of Hodder Headline Limited
338 Euston Road, London NW1 3BH

Copyright © Mick Inkpen 1998

ISBN 0 340 93061 6 (HB)

This edition produced exclusively for Bookstart in 2006.

A catalogue record for this book
is available from the British Library.
The right of Mick Inkpen to be identified as the author
of this work has been asserted by him in accordance with
the Copyright, Designs and Patents Act 1988.

Printed in Hong Kong
Colour Reproduction by Dot Gradations Ltd, U.K.

Splosh!

Mick Inkpen

Hodder
Children's
Books

A division of Hodder Headline Limited

'Splash!'
went the rain
on Kipper's umbrella.

'Splosh!' went the puddle as Kipper jumped into it.

'FLASH!' went
the lightning.
'BOOM!' went
the thunder.

'Drip, drip, drip,' went the water off the hedgehog's nose.

'Hop, squelch!
Hop, squelch!
Hop, squelch!'
went the three
little rabbits.

'AA A TISHOO!'
went the hedgehog.
And then he did it
again!
'ATISHOO!'

'Slop slap!
Slop slap!'
went the water
under the umbrella.

And at last,
without a slap,
or a slop, or a hop,
or a squelch, or a drip,
or a boom, or a flash
or a splosh,
or a splash. . .

. . . out came the sun!